POTTER

WALTER WANGERIN, JR.

Illustration

DANIEL SAN SOUCI

Augsburg
MINNEAPOLIS

This story and the memories

and the love in it

are dedicated to Virginia and Walter,

my parents forever.

POTTER
1994 Augsburg edition

Text copyright © 1985 Walter Wangerin, Jr. Illustrations copyright © 1985 Daniel San Souci.

Published in association with the literary agency of Alive Communications, P.O. Box 49068, Colorado Springs, CO 80949.

Cover and interior design: Patricia Boman

Library of Congress Cataloging-in-Publication Data

Wangerin, Walter.
    [Potter, come fly to the first of the earth]
    Potter / Walter Wangerin, Jr. ; illustration, Daniel San Souci. — 1994 Augsburg ed.
       p.   cm.
    Previously published as: Potter, come fly to the first of the earth. © 1985.
    Summary: Grief-stricken over a friend's drowning, Potter is visited by a bird who flies with him on a life-changing journey that helps him come to terms with sorrow and death.
    ISBN 0-8066-2775-1
    [1. Death—Fiction. 2. Grief—Fiction.]   I. San Souci, Daniel, ill.   II. Title.
PZ7.W1814Po   1994
[Fic]—dc20
                                            94-28924
                                               CIP
                                               AC

Manufactured in the U.S.A.   AF 9-2775

98 97 96 95 94   1 2 3 4 5 6 7 8 9 0

1

Three days, dear Jonathan. Three days is enough. Three days is too long for you to be gone. Come out! Come out! O Jonathan, come home again.

Potter knelt at the bedroom window, his elbows on the sill, his face in his hands, his eyes gone out to gaze over the yard and down the hill and to the woods at the bottom of that—and then the river. Adults were tramping the woods, but not Potter. Boats moved slowly upriver, and his own father was there, somewhere under the greening trees, kicking last autumn's leaves, but not Potter. That was wrong.

Potter should have been looking for Jonathan the same as everyone else, because who was the best friend of Jonathan? Potter. And who knew all of the places where they hid the summer long: woven huts, stone fireplaces, secrets stored in bottles and metal boxes? Potter. Who knew the exact color of Jonathan's red hair, and that he had white eyelashes and watery blue eyes and laughed like an ash can? Potter!

I could find you, Jonathan. I would say, Oh, there you are!

But Potter was not allowed to hunt for Jonathan. He knelt at the window, his forehead against the glass. Potter was not even allowed to leave the bedroom, and he should have been in bed, but he knelt at the window anyway. Potter was sick; he had a cough.

Winter always gave Potter this cough. He called it the Unstoppable Cough, and he plain got used to it, because what else could you do? The winter wind in Grand Forks, North Dakota, came straight and hard. And it was a drafty old house they lived in, 619 Reeves Drive, two stories. Through the weather, through the walls, through Potter's own chest and into his lungs the wind went, and there it curled like a worm, and there it stayed. When the worm moved, cold and down so deep, Potter coughed. The Unstoppable Cough. He would try to reach to the bottom of his lungs so that he could scrape that worm out. He would bark like a hound. But the worm was too deep. And then the cough would go on by itself, even when Potter didn't want to cough anymore. On and on, barking and bursting in his throat till all of his air was gone and his lungs had folded flat, but the cough went on anyway, silently, doubling him at the gut, shaking him and making his face swell up. That's why he called it the Unstoppable Cough.

That's why he was in his bedroom, second story, at the back of the house. His mother said that spring was as bad as winter, because you didn't know what the weather was going to do from one hour to the next, and he should have no fever at all for a week before he went outside. That's why Potter wasn't with Jonathan two days ago when he took his old red hair and went down the hill, laughing like the bang of an ash can, "Hah, Potter! Ho, Potter! Sixty-dollars-a-day, Potter!"

That's why he was pressing his forehead against the glass.

I could find you, Jonathan!

"No, Potter, absolutely not," his father had said.

And Potter had asked, "Why not?"

And his father had frowned as if he were in pain and whispered, "We don't want to lose you, too."

And that had scared Potter so much that he made his own face to go blank, as if he were saying, "So what? So what?"

But he was really afraid. And what was he afraid of? The river. So what was he staring at now while the evening darkened the hill, the woods, and the ravine? He couldn't see the people combing the ground below the trees. He couldn't see his father or Jonathan's father or Mr. Larson. So what was he staring at? Well, the river.

The Red River ran north. The only river to run north. In spring it swelled and grew furious and flooded, because it tried to get into Canada, but it ran against its own old winter ice, and was turned back, enraged. In spring the Red River split its sides, and this was a terrible thing. Into the woods it went, grabbing junk and timber, scouring the trees at their roots, and making a mud on which it was impossible to stand. Angry river. The north-flowing river, shut from its destination by its own cold self. Potter was watching the river and remembering what his father had said.

But Potter himself said, "Come out, come out. O Jonathan, come home again."

All at once a bird flew up and fluttered against the window, right at Potter's face. He screamed and jumped backward. For a moment the bird breasted the glass, as though trying to find a perch there. It was a red-winged, black bird. Then it flew back into the night.

Potter's whole body tingled, and his voice was gone, so that he couldn't answer when his mother called, "Potter? Potter? Are you all right?"

2

Just before noon on the following day, everyone stopped looking for Jonathan. They went home. Potter's father, too, came trudging up the hill until he stood on the level grass of the backyard. Potter saw him pause and glance up to the bedroom window. One glance. As soon as he noticed the face of Potter in the window, the man dropped his eyes, stiffened his back, and entered the house; and the screen door banged under Potter's knees.

Then the woods were empty altogether, though the river still chewed at the trees. It was a heavy sky, belly-down and smoky. It might rain later, but you never knew what the weather would do from one hour to the next. That's what his mother said.

Potter's father came into the bedroom. Potter turned and sat on his heels, but his father only looked at him for some time from frowning eyes, and making a hard pinch of his lips.

"Well," said Potter, "did everyone go to lunch, then?"

"I suppose so," said his father.

"Well, are we going to eat soon?"

"Mother will get you something," said his father.

"Aren't you going to eat?"

"No."

Potter lowered his voice. "Is it raining?" he asked.

"No," said his father.

"So," said Potter. He put his hands between his knees as if they were cold. He spoke so softly. "So, if you're not going to eat, and if it isn't raining, then why did you come in so soon?"

Potter's father had very strong forearms. When he folded his arms across his chest, the muscles stood out—and generally he folded his arms when he had nothing to say. Now Potter saw more clearly than ever these silent muscles, the power of his father, and he wished that all the power of his father would go around him in a hug. But he didn't ask for a hug, and his father didn't offer any. Too bad, too bad. Potter was beginning to think that he needed a hug.

His father said, "I came in to look at my son."

"Oh," said Potter. His lip trembled. "And then will you go out to look for Jonathan again?"

A bird began to flutter at Potter's window, thumping it. Up and down it went, up and down, and its beak made a ticking sound on the glass.

Potter's father looked at the bird instead of at Potter. "An Oriole wants in," he said.

"But will you go out to look for Jonathan again?" Potter said.

"Baltimore Oriole," said his father. And then, still without looking at Potter, he said, "No. Not again."

"Why?" said Potter. Somebody should say something straight out. Potter's lip was trembling. "Why?" But his father was better at folding his arms than at talking.

"No need," the man said, turning away. "No reason to."

It was when the bedroom door was shut that Potter began to cry. Not out loud. Simply, tears spilled and ran down his cheeks.

The Oriole was still fluttering at the window. Potter heard it and turned. An orange and burning bird.

"Go away," said Potter.

But at exactly that moment the bird began to sing in a clear, sliding whistle, as though calling to Potter through the glass.

"Go away! Go away!" cried Potter, hitting the sill with his fists.

The Oriole flew backward some feet, but then it returned with a stronger will and pecked and scratched the harder.

So Potter threw open the window and waved his arms. "Do you think I care?" he screamed. "Ha! I don't want to look at you! Ha! I don't want to hear you, old Baltimore Oriole. Just go away!"

The bird circled and flew to the elm which stood at the side of the yard, half again as high as the house. It was a lovely bird, both black and gold. But Potter slammed the window as though he hated it.

"Do you think I care?" he cried, shaking his finger at the Baltimore Oriole. "Do you think I care?" he whispered. This was a sentence that Potter suddenly wanted to say again and again.

His mother called him for lunch, and he hollered at the top of his lungs, "Do you think I care?" He sat down in the center of the bedroom floor. He folded his arms across his chest. He would holler it again, because when he was hollering he was not crying. He would holler it down the vent to his father in the kitchen below: "Do—"

But he did not holler it again. He heard his mother's voice instead, and he went very still, listening. He heard his father's voice answering, and he started to sob.

His mother said, "Ach, Martin, drowned? Drowned, just as you thought, poor boy?"

"Drowned," said his father. "But the body lingered on the riverbed, is why we couldn't find him."

"Oh!" his mother gasped. "But how—"

"Twig ran through his nose. It held him fast—"

Potter leaped up at that news. Potter spun round three times in the bedroom, as though he were lost, his hands at his ears. Then he drove through the door and down the hall to the top of the stairs.

"Potter, don't you come down here!" said his father at the bottom.

But Potter began to descend, his right hand on the banister.

"Jonathan!" cried Potter. "Jonathan, what did you do?" he cried, breathing harder and harder. Three steps from the bottom, he threw back his head and wailed, "I want to see my friend Jona—"

But then the worm twisted in his lungs, and Potter could talk no more. He began to cough great whooping barks, to cough and to cough till all of the air was out of him, and still the worm kept turning, and he coughed no air at all, hanging by one hand from the banister, his face two inches from the floor. But just before he fainted, the strong arms of his father slid under him and caught him, so he did not hit the hard wood.

Oh, Jonathan, Jonathan, who caught you?

3

The sky kept its promise, that day. Near evening the spring storms broke over the river and ripped the tops of the trees and slammed against Potter's house. It was wild weather from dusk and all through the night. But Potter was not in his bed. Neither was he in the house at all. He was in the back, under three trees.

After supper Potter's parents had left him alone. His mother woke him to see if he wanted to eat. He said, "Do you think I care?"

She said, "We're going to Jonathan's house for a while."

Potter didn't say anything to that, but lay abed with a terrible frown on his face. He folded his arms across his chest. His mother kissed his cheek and left. Potter didn't move. He didn't want to cry anymore, and moving might make him cry. He wanted to be angry. The trouble was, there was no one to be angry at. Not at his mother or his father, because it wasn't their fault. Not at Jonathan—he shouldn't be angry at Jonathan. He loved Jonathan. Jonathan was dead. That left two others. He could very easily be angry at God; but Potter was afraid of that, especially now. Or maybe Potter could be angry with Potter?

All at once there came a picking and a pecking at his window, and all at once Potter knew who he was angry at.

Potter sat up in bed and screamed at the top of his lungs, "Go away!"

The Baltimore Oriole was going up and down the window with its orange belly, the black beak pecking. Busy bird! Old busybody of a bird! It kept trying to come in.

Potter got up, waving his arms. He stomped his foot. "Do you think I care?" he screamed. It almost felt good to be so angry. "Go away, you Baltimore Oriole! Get away from me!"

But the bird was very willful. It never minded the commands of Potter; it kept flying bump against his window.

So Potter ran to the window and threw it open. The bird and the boy went backward from each other just an instant, one flying, one running. But then the bird perched directly on the windowsill, and Potter hated this with all his might. He picked up his baseball.

He cried out, "Don't you listen to me?" And he threw the baseball at the Oriole. And he hit it. And the bird fell down.

Potter went still, staring where the bird had been. He whispered, "Oh, no." Maybe he would cry for sure, now. There was no anger left in Potter, no anger at all. "Oh, no, no."

But it was right then that the first winds of the storm began to blow, whipping the backs of the trees and rushing Potter's bedroom, too. Enormous raindrops, eight or twelve of them, bombed the windowpanes, and Potter's heart was turned inside of him.

Potter put his head out of the window. He searched the ground for the Oriole. "Don't die," he said. "I didn't mean it." And then he called against the wind, "O Baltimore Oriole, where are you?"

Poor Potter's lip was trembling. He had such pain in his chest for the thing he had done, and he was alone besides! And this was a dangerous storm. So down the stairs went Potter, through the kitchen, out the back door; and down again went Potter to his hands and his knees; under the bushes he went, and his pajama shirt blew up to his neck.

"Where are you, Baltimore Oriole?"

There it was, lying on its side. Its eye was closed.

Potter picked it up, making a crib of his two hands, and kissed it. "But I love you," he said. "O Baltimore Oriole, what did I do? Don't die. Don't go away like Jonathan went away. I'm so sorry," said the boy, "and I love you."

How thin was the bird's neck, no thicker than matchsticks! Why did God make their necks so thin? Didn't he know how easily they could die? Potter felt the feathers on his upper lip, so soft at the breast of the bird—and then his nose was tweaked.

He stopped kissing the bird.

"Did you do that to me, Baltimore Oriole?" he said holding his breath. Its black eye was open. They looked at each other a moment, and then the bird reached out its beak and distinctly, for the second time, tweaked the nose of Potter.

"Oh, dear Baltimore Oriole," whispered Potter, "you are alive. I am so glad." He gazed at the bird.

But now this boy, crouching underneath the bushes at the back of his house, did a strange thing. Although he was relieved to be twice kissed by the bird, he began to cry. Potter couldn't stop his tears anymore, but sobbed and sobbed and held the bird so carefully. Like a little wolf he opened his mouth and wailed to the winds.

And what he said was, "Baltimore Oriole, I am so lonely." He said, "Why do the good friends die? Why couldn't I be dead instead of Jonathan? Oh, oh, I am so lonely!"

The bird moved in his hands. It stood up on the wrist of Potter and cocked its head left and right as though it were watching a curious sight, a boy with his mouth wide open. It was a beautiful bird.

So Potter wept, "It's no good, dear Baltimore Oriole. How could you be my friend if you can't talk and I can't understand you? Birds can't be Jonathans. I hate Adam," Potter said. "If Adam didn't sin then we could be friends. But this is the way that it is. Birds," sobbed Potter, "birds can't know my feelings. You don't know how sad this world is—"

But then the most wonderful thing happened. Potter looked and saw in the Oriole's eye a tear, a single tear of perfect sadness as the bird gazed back at the boy.

Potter whispered, "You too?"

Suddenly lightning split the heavens apart, arcing from Minnesota to North Dakota, and thunder punched the lungs of Potter. Like nerves aflame the lightning scorched the sky. The wind got up in a furious roar, and now the rain soaked the earth for sure.

"You too?" The boy was filled with gratitude. "Do you see why I love you so much?" he shouted. "And I'll protect you, Baltimore Oriole!"

Potter covered the Oriole in his pajama shirt, and squinted through this wild weather, and ran to the woods. He found a hollow among the roots of three trees, where the wind was weaker and the raindrops dripped but did not sting. He was coughing, now—what he called his Unstoppable Cough. No matter to that: he had a friend, someone to watch out for, and this was the place where he and Jonathan used to hide, a good place. Like a bear cub he curled himself down, the Oriole between his knees and his chest.

Potter was coughing.

One finger of Potter was stroking the head of the Oriole.

Finally, Potter fell asleep.

Jonathan, will you come and play with me tomorrow?

When his father went out with a high-powered searchlight and found the boy, Potter was still smiling. But he had developed a fever. His hands were folded. And his father didn't understand what Potter had done, because there was no bird there anymore.

"Why?" said his father when he picked him up. The strong man sounded angry. "Potter, Potter, why?"

4

How many days and nights did Potter lie sick after that? He didn't know, nor did he try to count them. Time was squeezing and stretching in front of him like pictures on a rubber balloon.

Potter was hot. His tongue stuck like clay in his mouth. But then Potter would tremble helplessly, frozen colder than the Red River at its Canadian mouth. He drew his knees to his chest, shuddering. But then Potter would throw his covers aside, strip to his underpants, and lie spread-eagle on the sheets, gulping air.

Potter moaned.

His mother came in and put damp cloths on his forehead.

His father stood in the doorway with his arms folded.

He said, "Potter, why?"

It sounded to Potter as though his father were roaring, a very angry man. Potter couldn't answer him. He didn't know what the man was asking. He could only moan.

His father said, "Why did you go out in the rain? What? Did you want to follow Jonathan?"

Follow Jonathan.

"Hush, Martin!" his mother cried, grabbing the boy. "You oughtn't say such a thing ever—not ever!" And that was all his father said. He left the room. But his mother rocked Potter, talking the loveliest things and singing lullabies as he had never heard them before.

Potter—Potter only moaned.

For what was real, and what wasn't? When was he awake, and when was he asleep? All the world went sliding in his poor head. He could not tell truly

whether his eyes were open and he saw, or whether they were closed and he dreamed. Powerful were the dreams in him during those days.

This was a very sick Potter.

Then he noticed that the singing of his mother had changed. In the deep, invisible darkness it rose to a lightsome whistle: *Dee-dit, dah-der, dee-dit,* over and over again, appealing to the sweet soul of the boy and causing him to weep for the very beauty of the sound. *Dee-dit, dah-der, dee-dit.*

Once, while the wonderful melody filled his ears, he felt a fine breeze across his face, a wind so cool that it blew the fever from his forehead.

Mother, are you fanning me? he asked.

His mother did not answer him; but the song still trembled in the bedroom, and he looked, and he saw above him on the bedstead the Baltimore Oriole. See? The window was open! And see? The bird was straking its two wings through the air making such a gentle breeze and singing this song: "Dee-dit, dah-der, dee-dit."

Well, said Potter, reaching up his hand and smiling, *so you came back after all. I knew that you would come back, my friend.*

But before his hand could reach as high as the Oriole, Potter was sleeping again—more peacefully than ever since Jonathan had gone.

But other nights and other darknesses were different from this one.

Potter would get out of bed crying, *Jonathan! Jonathan!* He crawled on the floor looking for his friend. Under the bed? No, not there. What would Jonathan be doing under the bed. Behind the door? In the closet? No, no. Outside? Outside! Waiting to play!

Jonathan! Potter called as he crawled to the window, aching with loneliness. *Jonathan, where are you now?*

But Potter's mother would come saying, "Hush, Potter. O my Potter, hush." And she would hold him to her breast, and Potter would say, *Red hair is too real to die.* She would shake her head and say, "God wanted Jonathan to come be home with him in heaven. Hush, Potter. You'll only break your heart to think on things that cannot be."

If God took Jonathan away from me, said Potter, *then I hate God.* But maybe his mother didn't hear what he said, because she went on rocking him and saying, "God came and took your friend—"

Then Potter looked over his mother's shoulder and saw the Baltimore Oriole perched outside the window. And behold, the bird understood! The Oriole was weeping just as Potter himself was weeping. No words. No talk of God. No song. But open eyes and tears.

O my friend! cried Potter. *I'm so glad to see you!*

Potter stretched out his arms and tried to get up. He struggled against his mother. She could barely restrain him, for the desire to hold the Oriole again was very strong in him.

"Martin!" screamed his mother. "Martin, help me!"

So his father came and took the boy by his shoulders. His father was too, too strong. Immediately his mother shut the window.

Mama! Potter wailed like a wolf cub. *Mama, don't!*

She knelt beside him. She was crying, too. "My poor, poor Potter," she said, "please hush and let it all come right."

But Potter pulled his knees up to his chest and pretended to be sleeping. When his parents left the room, the child arose with terrible pain and dizziness and went to the window and gritted his teeth and opened it a crack. Then he fell upon the bed again.

He was only a boy. Nevertheless, with the weight of a great elm tree he toppled down in tiredness.

5

—————

Eat it, Potter, eat it."

Potter popped open his eyes. Nighttime. He was wide awake and lost. He thought that he had been coughing, but he wasn't coughing now, and things were cold and clear around him. The boy held still, lest he fall off something. He turned his eyes left and right, and there was the dresser, his dresser, three drawers closed and one stuck out like a tongue; and there was his desk and the lamp lit dim and his books and pencils; and, yes, that was the place he used to sit reading *Jerry Todd* and Hans Andersen and Ovid; and here were his own covers kicked low, and there was the window still open its crack: Potter's room. This was Potter's bedroom—not so strange after all. But it had never been so sharp to his seeing before, as though he were Potter in a flash photograph.

"Eat it, Potter, eat it."

He lay naked, except for his underpants. The sky was deep green outside his window, the horizon black. The river would be the deepest thing in that horizon, like a slash, a cut in the earth, like a snake belly-down forever north, forever south and silent and sliding and terrible, and Potter hated it.

Suddenly something dropped to the sheet beside him. Now he turned his head, and there was the Baltimore Oriole, not two feet from his face. Potter smiled immediately. The Oriole bowed and said, "Dee-dit, dah-der, dee-dit," nodding and bowing low.

Oh, hello, Baltimore Oriole, said Potter. He moved his hand to touch the bird, but it hopped just out of reach and he was a very slow boy in his sickness.

The bird spoke again, still nodding; but this time Potter's eyes widened and his mouth dropped open. The bird said, "Dee-dit, Potter, eat it. Eat it, Potter, eat it."

Poor Potter. The heart in the boy began to beat with dangerous violence, and his temples ached. *Oh, no!* he cried. *What are you doing? Did you hear what you just said, Baltimore Oriole?* The boy put his hands to his cheeks. *You said my name! Oh, no! And besides that, I understood you. O dear Baltimore Oriole, what are we doing? We're talking!*

Poor Potter. He felt that he was going to cry again, this time for fear.

The best things in the world are treasures. But treasures might be lost or stolen. Didn't Potter know as much on account of Jonathan? And here was the most splendid treasure of all, hardly to be believed, that he and the bird might be friends, talking, talking, passing the time of day. So if this were really true, how terrifying to think that he could lose this, too!

But the Oriole was not dismayed. The Oriole had business to do, and do it the beautiful bird did. It fluttered to the toe of Potter and perched there. This tickled the boy. Next it flew to his chest and put its black eye, by a half cock, directly in front of Potter's face. "Eat it, Potter, eat it," it said, nodding with the sternest authority. Then it jumped to the sheet and picked in one claw three silken leaves and held them up and repeated the command, "Eat it, Potter, eat it."

Potter held his breath, watching. Potter didn't budge a muscle.

So the Oriole laid one leaf on his left hand and one leaf on his right and one leaf—while poor Potter crossed his eyes—lightly on his lips.

"Mugwort, Potter," the bird announced, proud of itself. "Eat muggins in May. You eat it, Potter. Eat it."

Slowly, Potter put out his tongue. The leaf stuck to it like a feather. All at once the Oriole touched its head beneath a wing and made a tiny sound like sneezing: *ker-poop!*

But that was no sneeze, and Potter knew it. Even to a bird, a cross-eyed boy with his tongue stuck out looked silly. The Baltimore Oriole was laughing.

"Pretty Potter! Pretty Potter! *Ker-Poop!*"

Potter, in spite of himself, said, *Hee-hee!* Next, he giggled, and from giggling he went to chuckling. So then they were friends together, laughing together—and that made all the difference. Right easily the boy began to chew the mugwort, and the one in his left hand, and the one in his right, all three, a cheerful little snack.

But then the game that had begun funny turned very, very serious.

Bitter were the mugwort leaves. Spit flooded Potter's mouth, and his eyes ran tears, and he swallowed. Then his nostrils flared, the better to breathe, and his whole body went to tingling, and a great lump formed in his stomach where the bitter oils had run.

Nobody was laughing now.

Baltimore Oriole, Potter gasped, *what is happening to me?*

From far away and solemnly the Oriole sang his song, "Eat it, Potter, eat it."

Potter's stomach tightened and his mouth opened up, as though to vomit. His skinny muscles contracted around the lump, pushing it forward, and he thought that he would suffocate when it came to his throat.

Ba, Ba, Baltimore! he cried, frightened. He was such a small boy.

Potter's mouth yawned as wide as a cave, and his throat went vastly hollow, and the lump squeezed higher and higher, and then he threw back his head. He arched his spine in a spasm. But he could not scream anymore, because the lump was coming.

He heard the Oriole calling, "Push, Potter, push!"

Potter pushed. He wanted to breathe. He was dying, the huge lump jammed at the back of his tongue—

Then suddenly came the most amazing change. All at once Potter was *in* a cave, rising from the deepest reaches of the earth. He was being pushed out of a damp, dark hole to air and to freedom. With strong scratchings of his feet he climbed, and he cried, *Wait for me! Wait for me!*

Potter wasn't dying at all. He was being born.

At the mouth of the cave hung stalactites like teeth, and like teeth the stalagmites stood up. Potter crawled between them. His head felt a cool breeze, and how grateful he was to breathe again! Then his shoulders and his back and his stomach squeezed out—and he was free.

And behold! Here was the Baltimore Oriole beside him, a definite twinkle in both its eyes and warm words singing: "Welcome, Potter, welcome." But the bird was now exactly the size of Potter himself! They were the same.

But everything else was different. His bedroom had grown enormous, his dresser as big as a four-story house, his desk was a mesa, his bed was a wilderness.

Potter said to the Oriole, *Friends?* He figured he needed a friend to trust in if the world was going to swell and surprise him.

And then it was a blessing that the Oriole answered, "Friends, dear Potter," because the next sight was a shock.

There, on his back in the center of the bed, lay a little boy, naked except for his underpants, his eyes rolled up, his mouth wide open.

That's me! Potter cried, running backward. *That's Potter there!*

How skinny was that body, how pale and helpless. Potter wanted to cry for what he saw.

But the Oriole came and kissed his neck. "Shhh, Potter," said the Oriole. "This is you here, somebody that I'm kissing. This is the soul of you, set free. And I set you free for a reason, a very good reason. Oh, Potter, come ride the wind with me."

I came out of my mouth, said Potter, still staring at the little boy.

"Aye," said the Oriole orange. "To soar the sky with me."

I—I left my self behind.

"Aye. To learn the holy things of God, because you asked me."

Baltimore Oriole, Potter whispered as though they were in church, *am I dead?*

"Nay, Potter," laughed the Oriole gentle. "Nay, and never more alive. Oh, Potter, look at yourself. You are a bird, now."

Indeed. He was a bird. A dumpy sort of bird, to be sure, a little head on a lumpish body, doughy at the breast of him, his wings crossed at his lower back, and a song, when he sang, so mournful as to break your heart—but a bird nevertheless.

"A dove," said the Oriole. "Oh, come on, Potter, Dove-Potter. Come fly with me!"

Straightway the Oriole twitted to the window and was gone.

Well, that left a lonely bedroom and the smell of sickness, and Potter did not want to stay there. So he followed. He waddled across the bedroom floor, thrusting his head forward like a chicken. He jumped to the windowsill, and without a second thought he slipped into the night.

23

Ooooooooooooooriole! screamed Potter. He was falling like an open sheet.

"Wings, Potter!" cried the Oriole. "Open your wings!"

He did. And what happened then was a wonder of the mighty God and a gift to Potter forever.

When just above the bushes his wings went out, they caught the air like sheaves of wheat beneath his shoulders, and suddenly he was sailing level to the ground at an easy speed.

Potter began to laugh. He tightened a muscle above his butt; his tail fanned forward, and he soared up. Mighty flaps of his wings—clumsy flaps, since the wing tips slapped above and below his body—powerful flaps, and he arose. He lunged higher and higher. Up the side of the house; up so high he cleared the elm; up and up and loose and free until the city lights turned below him, the river a ribbon of darkness, the woods like fur on the back of a bear.

Potter gulped the glory of God, the goodness of creation, and all of heaven stretched around him. He laughed like a loon, a little crazy to have let go of the earth, to float at the tops of the clouds.

Ha, ha! Swoop to the left, Dove-Potter, why not? He did. And swoop to the right, you light-hearted bird. He did. Then dive, child, dive like a hawk straight down from the clouds, your feathers thrumming at such high speeds, your eyes made narrow by streaking the winds. He did. He did: like an arrow piercing down to the earth and whistling the wind, he did!

Suddenly: "Potter!"

The name came from behind his head. He stumbled in the air, tumbled, and hit the ground. He bounced. Oh, awkward, to be on one's feet again.

"Potter," said the Oriole, "this has been good, and I laughed when you laughed, and your gladness has made me glad. But you have to go back to you again."

This is so wonderful, Baltimore Oriole, said Potter, full of chatter. *I never knew that I could be so light. Why don't we tell all the children—*

"Potter! Your mother is soon to look in on you—"

And what will I do? I'll tell her about flying.

"Please, Potter, you don't understand. When she sees the body-you, she will think that you are dead."

Dead? Coldness shot through Potter's body, and the night was dark after all, and his little window at the second floor glowed orange. *Dead?* Oh, the sad earth!

"And she will cry," said the Oriole.

Mama! My mama!

"Up, now, Potter. Come up for the love of your mother."

Quickly, then, they flew to the ledge of his bedroom window, and they entered in. Potter looked at himself, the sickly boy with his mouth wide open and his back twisted. Potter felt sorry for him. But then he saw himself in the way that his mother might see him: thin legs, thin arms, no motion in her son, no greeting in his eyes, and he hurt for her. What would his mother say, if she saw no life in Potter?

Therefore, Potter-the-bird went up to the mouth of Potter-the-boy and prepared to climb down the cave again. Down the damp hole, down the dark he would go, on account of his mother, down to the bottom of clay and buried—

Suddenly Potter was afraid. He turned to the Oriole, still perched on the windowsill.

Friends? he pleaded.

"Friends," said the Oriole.

I won't lose you, please, the way that I lost Jonathan?

"Oh, Potter, this is just the beginning," said the Oriole. "There is a reason why I brought you out of yourself. I will show you what's become of Jonathan—"

He drowned, said Potter.

"Hush. Hush that, Potter," said the Oriole. "And this is the reason: because you held me, child of Adam, and because you loved me."

So Potter remembered the promise. He put his head into his mouth and struggled down his throat with trouble. There came the moment when he thought he could not breathe: the bird was smothered and the boy was choking. But that moment passed when he broke into a long, long cough, and his boy's body rolled over on the bed, wracked with his terrible coughing.

His mother came in and took his head between her hands. Potter wept to feel the coolness of her hands. He grabbed them and held on with all his might.

"My poor, poor baby," she said.

Oh, Mama, Mama.

The coughing ended, finally, leaving Potter all exhausted and covered with sweat. But he smiled a little smile at her, for he loved her and he loved touching her, and there was a part of him that had never been so happy.

"I think you had a nightmare, Potter," she said.

But the Oriole sang in the morning dusk, "Dee-dit, dah-der, dee-dit."

6

In the days when Potter was a boy and sick, the doctors did not have penicillins for healing, no shots to shoot the fever down. Therefore, children had to fight fevers with the strength of their own small bodies, and often no one knew who'd be the stronger, the boy or the fever. If the boy, then the fever went away. But if the fever, then they both departed to the everlasting cold, zero at the bone.

A boy could die.

And there was a name for the worst period of the disease. When the boy and the fever fought each other the hardest—when they wrestled desperately to death or to health again—that was called the "crisis." Parents agonized during the "crisis." They couldn't sleep. They sat by their child, praying, wiping his forehead in cool cloths, wishing that they could fight the fiery enemy for him and sad that they could not. Parents paced in their kitchens under yellow light bulbs, deep at night. They drank coffee. Sometimes they just stared at one another, as though someone might say something magical and their child would come downstairs yawning and asking for a drink of water. But no. They wouldn't say anything at all. There was nothing magical to say. What they did during the "crisis" was, they waited.

The "crisis" might last for three hours before the child sighed and slipped into a deeper sleep of one sort or another: three hours, seven hours, thirteen hours.

Potter's "crisis" lasted three days. Ah, Potter! He was such a skinny child.

It began the evening after his mother had said, "You had a nightmare." She was closing the curtains in his room and she was just about to shut the window, too, when Potter said right clearly, "It's too tight."

"What, baby?" said his mother, smiling, one hand on the sash.

"It's too tight," said Potter.

And this is why his mother was smiling: Potter had no covers on. No pajamas. Nothing was tight on him. He was acting silly, and that made his mother glad. "Go to sleep, rapscallion," she said.

But the boy suddenly burst into the most desolated howl. Oh, the lonely wolf cub! No one understood his sorrow. "It's too tight! It's too tight! Mama, it's too *tight!*" wailed Potter.

"What, baby? What's too tight?" His mother wasn't smiling, now, but perplexed. She stepped toward his bed. His eyes were closed. "Are you sleeping," she whispered, "and dreaming after all?"

Potter said, "My body." He turned and howled, "My *body* is too tight on me!"

She didn't understand this saying, but neither did she try to. For when she came to Potter's bed, and when she touched his forehead, she was terrified.

"Martin!" she shrieked. She had never screamed like that before. She had never been so scared. "Martin! Martin! Potter's burning up!" Then she mumbled, "Potter, oh, Potter, Potter, Potter," feeling his cheeks with her own cheek, sliding her hands all down his body. "MARTIN! HURRY!"

Paper dry was Potter's skin. His face, forehead, and throat were red as flame. The bridge of his nose was white. He was breathing breaths no deeper than a sparrow's, tiny, tiny puffs of nothing.

"My body is. Too tight for. Me."

"He's delirious," Potter's mother chattered when his father strode in. "I think that he is one hundred and six degrees. Oh, Martin! A fever this high could ruin his brain. You know, you know. A fever like this could stop his—Oh, Martin!"

Potter's father said nothing at all. But, smelling of wood, his strong arms covered with sawdust, he lifted his son into the air and bore him from the room.

Potter remembered forever the smell of wood as the smell of the nearness of God; and the feel of sawdust on his cheek was the stuff of love. Whenever thereafter the saws would cut to the heart of the white pine, Potter would fall silent and whisper in his soul, "Ah, this is sacred."

So down the stairs went Potter in the cradle of his father's arms, thin legs swinging. In the kitchen the man gathered the whole boy under one arm. With the other he dragged a steel tub from under the sink. He attached a hose to the faucet, then shot water into the tub—all in a few seconds. He was very stern. He was very strong.

The water foamed and swirled beneath its steady jet. Potter's father breathed through his nose, which whistled.

Potter's mother said, "I'm going to Larsons. I'll ask them to get the doctor. They'll do that. I'll be back."

His mother could not stand still.

The steel tub swelled with water. Potter's father went down on his knees beside it, his son straight out in front of him, held almost like a tender prayer, or sacrifice. And then the man let the boy by inches sink into the water.

It was so cold! Potter thrashed with his arms and sucked air. He hit his father hard on the lip, and the lip began to bleed, but his father did not move a whit and the boy didn't know what he had done. He was just shocked by the freezing water. His scalp and neck and skin all shriveled on his body.

And while he was in the water, he woke up. He looked and he saw his father's face all covered with sawdust and pain, and this was a new thing for the boy, a most curious thing, for he had never seen his father in pain before, never before in pain.

"Are you all right, Poppi?" he asked.

His father nodded.

"Did you know that you are bleeding?"

His father shook his head, but he did nothing to wipe the red run of blood from his chin, because both his arms were under Potter.

So Potter stuck out his pointer finger and dabbed the blood away, and sawdust and whisker-grit were in that dab. And when he felt the stiffness of his father's whiskers, Potter said, "I love you, Poppi."

Immediately the mouth of Potter's father drew tight, and white went his face, and hard his eyes, and frowning his brow. Potter's father neither looked at him nor said a word, but that was okay with Potter. Potter was used to his father by now.

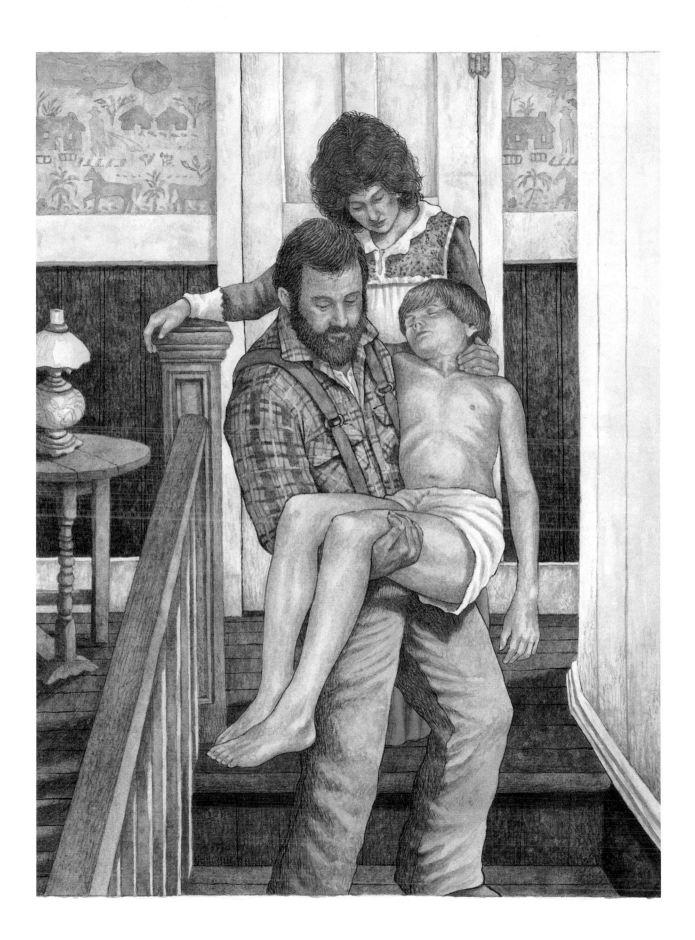

Then Potter sighed and seemed to fall asleep, resting his head on his father's shoulder.

In a little while his mother came back. Right behind her Mrs. Larson bustled in with the biggest butt in all the world and great arms that could never hang straight down because, like the sides of pyramids, they had to make room for Mrs. Larson's bottom, seventeen feet from one side to the other. Mrs. Larson had enormous quantities of sympathy, had gallons of pity, whole oceans of compassion— and she kept it all inside her butt. That's what Jonathan said.

When Mrs. Larson wanted to help the weak, the heavy laden, cumbered with a load of care, no man could stop her, and it didn't matter the time, night or midnight. Look out for Mrs. Larson, when she came to heal you! And how did she heal you? She cooked. She baked. She boiled and fried and diced. She measured and whipped and covered the kitchen in flour and generally caused food to happen everywhere.

This she began to do the instant that she saw Potter in his tub, so the kitchen was full of Mrs. Larson.

Soon the doctor came as well, and after him came Mr. Larson with a raw, red face, and then who could move in such a crowd? Who could breathe?

The doctor examined Potter. "Yep. The 'crisis,'" he said. "You'll have to watch him, now. Keep water in your tub. If he can swallow, give him liquids. Liquids—that's the order of the day. Fluids till his nostrils dribble—"

Mrs. Larson switched at once from cakes to broth.

Mr. Larson looked superficial. He didn't know where to put his hands. He didn't know where to put himself. He always followed Mrs. Larson.

Potter's mother felt duty-bound to care for all these people.

But Potter's father did not.

When the boy was cool, it didn't matter who was talking, who was cooking, or who was drinking coffee. The man rose up with his son raining water all over the floor, and he left the kitchen. He wrapped the boy in a towel and carried him to his bedroom and dried him with vigorous rubbings all over his body, and Potter opened his eyes again.

Potter smiled. He liked this touch of his father.

Potter's father saw that and began to clear his throat with much violence, and then he did an extraordinary thing.

He said, "Can you hear me?"

Potter said, "Yes, Poppi."

"And do you remember what you said downstairs?" he asked.

Potter said, "Yes, Poppi."

"Well," said his father, blinking rapidly, "I feel the same way, too, Potter."

Immediately the man stood straight up and folded his arms across his chest and put a fierce look on his face. And Potter laughed.

Oh, Potter knew what it cost his father to say such a thing. Potter knew the wonder that had just taken place, for Potter had never, never heard his father to hint at love before. How dearly he wanted to pay his father back for such a kindness. But what did he have to give him? Ah, Poppi! Then Potter grinned, for he thought that he would tell his father his secret, this for his father alone.

"I can fly," he said.

Potter's father nodded.

"This is true," said Potter. "I can fly. I flied yesterday sometime. I went out that window, and I was very happy. Poppi, I wasn't sick at all. The Unstoppable Cough was gone."

Potter noticed the bit of a smile at his father's lips and kind eyes crinkling down on him. This made Potter's heart to rejoice, because he was giving his father some happiness, too. So he chattered on, telling more and more.

"Do you remember the Baltimore Oriole at my window, yes? Well, he comes back, you see. He is my friend. He comes in the crack there. He talks with me in English, and I am a dove, and we go out the window together—"

The man's smile faded. He glanced at the window, a gathering frown on his forehead. But Potter's tongue was loose, and he went on.

"You think the tree is high? Ho, I flied a hundred times higher than that. And this is just the beginning, Poppi. I'm going out the window again, because the Oriole promised it to me, and we are going to follow Jonathan, to find out where he went. I'm going to find my dear friend Jonathan—Poppi? Poppi? *Oh, Father, no!*" cried the boy.

For his father had left him. The man had suddenly turned from his son and had gone to the window and had shut it with an absolute bang. Then he turned round to Potter with a very angry face.

"Jonathan is dead," he said.

"I know," said Potter.

"Drowned," said the man. Potter's eyes began to sting with tears.

"I know," he said.

"But not you! Not you, Potter!"

Potter said, "Why are you so angry?"

"You, Potter, are not going to die. Do you hear me?"

In his mind the boy said, *I hear you.* But all he could do out loud was to cry, for both the sadness and the fever were catching him away again, stealing Potter, the one like an eagle, the other a rook.

"Potter!" The nostrils of his father were flaring. Oh, why was he so angry? "Potter, you are my son." His eyes were red, were wet. "You will forget this following of Jonathan—"

Open the window, Father, Potter said. *Please, Poppi, open the window so that the Baltimore Oriole could come in again. Please.*

But his father did not so much as look at the window under his great thunderclap of a frown. He was squeezing his eyes shut. He left the room.

Potter was alone.

Then the fever attacked him again, and they began to wrestle. Life and death. Life or death. Potter had entered his "crisis."

7

Potter began to pray. He got the idea from his mother. This poor lady prayed endless prayers around Potter these days, stroking and stroking his hair.

She prayed: "Mighty God, O let me have my child some little longer, yet. Don't take him from me. I will be so empty if you take my boy away from me. And what could you want with a child who has done nothing yet? Neither greatness nor sinning is in my Potter. He hasn't had the time. So what kind of a God would you be to give and to take so quickly? It would be a terrible mistake. And how, and how—" She trembled with her prayer. "And how could I love you if you snatched my Potter from my house?"

But Potter prayed: *Let me follow Jonathan. Please let me see what happened to my friend Jonathan. O God, I know why I am sick. Because it isn't finished yet. Not until, not until—*

This was Potter's prayer. But it all came out in a single word. The boy would throw his head to the left and to the right and howl at the top of his lungs: "Jonathan!"

Deep under the river, wreathed in a flowing riverweed, rolling with the current of cold waters, was a boy. His mouth was open. Little fishes darted through his cloud of ruddy hair. And one crooked twig, like a witch's finger, came out of the mud and caught him at the nostril.

"Jonathaaaaaan!"

It was a horrible sight.

It had to be canceled, done away with forever, abolished, forgotten, atoned, forgiven, *answered!* Or else Potter could never live in peace again.

"Oh, God! Oh, Jonathaaaaaan!"

Potter woke up with his own voice still circling the air of his bedroom. He was panting like a dog in August, sweat running the whole of his skinny body. His hair was matted to his forehead, and he stank. He was alone.

Two birds fluttered at the window. The Oriole, its beak full of leaves, bumped glass like a tennis ball. Very urgent, it was, and Potter knew that the time had come.

The other bird was black in every respect, except with red at its shoulders. It was as skillful on the wing as the Oriole; but it shied from the glass, from the window and the house. It hadn't the boldness of its companion.

Potter looked at them and shook his head. His mouth was yanked back at the corners, as if grinning. But he wasn't grinning. He was trying not to cry. It seemed to him that his friend was calling, and he could not answer. It seemed to him that the bird was going away forever and with it the joy of Jonathan. It seemed to him that holiness was on the other side of the window, and the window was locked.

Potter hid his face in the pillow.

Go *away,* he said.

Then he heard the dear song of the bird: "Eat it, Potter, eat it," and that made his soul to ache for loneliness.

Oh! Oh, please, wept Potter, *I cannot go!*

But an insistent drumming was set up at the window. The Oriole pecked like seconds on a clock, as light as cottonwood. And with such loving the Oriole called, "Here, dear! Come right here!"

So Potter, still holding the pillow in front of his face, got up from bed. A swooning swept over him, and he veered to the left, and he would have fainted, except that the pecking called him, the pecking focused him, and he stumbled blindly to the pecking. He gasped. He bowed his head and toppled forward. Pillow and head, he hit the window, which shattered raining glass adown the bushes. And Potter slumped to the floor.

Straightway the Oriole was at his side, and the leaves were pressed against his lips. As though he were an infant with his mouth agape, he let the Oriole feed him, for he had no strength to help. He chewed the bitter leaves. He swallowed

37

the bitter oils, and the lump arose in his gut again, and the spasms grabbed and pushed it forward. How pitifully his skinny stomach squeezed the lump! How weakly it climbed to his throat. But it came.

And soon Potter, the soul of Potter, lightsome, bright and glorious, sprang free of his own stiff self. He shook his feathers like metal foil.

Here I am, said Potter the dove. He was breathless, laughing.

"All in good time, good Potter," said the Oriole, more beautiful than ever before, golden, black, and shining. "All in good time."

Friends? said Potter.

"Friends," said the Oriole. "Quickly, let's go."

And by double swoops above the body of a boy, by flight through a broken window they went.

8

Potter, you shouldn't hate your body."

This is what the Baltimore Oriole said when they had flown some time at the top of the sky, streaking beneath the firmament. Potter flew beside it, mystified by the endless, easy beating of his own wings and by the roundness of the earth below and by the silence. But this was no lonely silence, for the thoughts of the stars were everywhere here, and they thought in melody.

East, east and south the bird and Potter flew, a half a continent in darkness when heaven was bright and peopled but America was black: two friends too high for anyone to know their passage, two birds free. Then the morning rushed toward them and they were above the ocean, its waters first golden in the dawning, then brassy by the sunlight, and then aluminum at noon. Sometimes clouds, like angels' breath, blew backward underneath their bellies, so that Potter wondered at his speed; but never did he tire. Nor ever did he cease to exalt in the winds that lifted him.

Baltimore Oriole, I do not hate my body, he called. *I feel sorry for it. It can't fly.*

"Oh, it can fly higher than I," cried the Oriole, "by thinking alone. Just by thinking. It can think the galaxies, dear Potter my brother; and then, by two swift thoughts, it has gone to travel among them."

But it coughs, Baltimore Oriole, and it is sick. Poor skinny ribs, poor naked knees still bunched on my bedroom floor! How could anyone like that little dishrag—a boy?

"I do," called the Oriole. "I envy the body of a boy."

You? Beautiful Baltimore Oriole, I cry to see your freedom and to hear your song. Why should you wish you were me?

"Ah, Potter, Potter! When God came down to live among the creatures of the earth, did he stop in the sky and become a bird? Nay, but he was born of a woman and he became a human being. Pish, but I think there's a dummy in Potter."

On and on they flew, caught in a headlong wind that took the miles like a snake's tongue, darting.

"This is the Brave Westerly," called the Oriole.

Who is? Potter saw no one about.

"The wind whose back we are riding."

Oh, said Potter. *Hello, Brave Westerly,* he said.

A frowning crag of land crawled toward them through the ocean. To this they descended. On its massive forehead they rested, and the wind went on without them for a while.

Potter said, *What is this place?*

The Oriole answered, "The end of the earth. A rock, Potter."

Does he have a name, too?

"Gibraltar."

Hello, Gibraltar, said Potter. He was happy and excited, and you never knew: anything at all might want to be the friend of a bird—now that Potter was a bird.

High above them, far ahead of them, Potter saw a dot in the sky, and he thought it was the canny black bird, red at the shoulder, which was a surprise to him, that this fellow would be going in the same direction as they were going. How nice!

Potter turned to the Oriole to ask about this, but the Oriole had already launched itself into the air, crying, "Up, Potter, up. If you are to see the whole of the story, we've got to get there first, before the night!"

Now they crossed a sea so azure and so clear that the hills and the valleys underwater lay like a map beneath their seeing.

"Five hundred years," sang the Oriole a misty song: "Once with every half one thousand years, the story of God takes place for us, and the birds are reminded, and the birds remember. The birds know the love of God. Hurry, Potter, that you might see the story. Hurry, my brother, that you might know it, too—"

Like a blazing bullet, a tracer, the Oriole sped ahead, and together they shot over land, leaving the sea behind. This was yellow desert, windswept and blistered, blown into the yawning shapes of desolation: lonely land, dry for miles around, a wilderness.

"There!" cried the Oriole, nearly bursting with anticipation. Potter grinned. His friend had never been so giddy before. "There! There! Do you see him, Potter?"

But the sun behind them was so low that it made streaks of deep purple across the desert, shadows that swallowed the sight. Potter saw nothing.

"Oh, Potter! Dear Potter, look! Just once in a hundred times five! Look! The Phoenix!"

Felix? said Potter, squinting.

He saw an island of greensward in the middle of the wilderness, and in the middle of that a fountain of trees, some of them high, one of them higher than all the others, leaning and hanging its leaves like the hair of a woman. Palm trees.

Suddenly, *Felix!* screamed Potter. *I see him!*

Oh, the magnificent bird that Potter saw, sinking down upon the tallest tree! Potter felt tiny at that size, as great as an eagle's, and the colors of the creature dazzled his eyes: gold at the neck, deep purple for the rest of his body, a tail azure-blue inmixed like a king's robe with feathers of rose, and his head was set with a crest most curiously wrought.

Little Potter and the gladsome Oriole perched in a lesser tree, held very still, and watched.

The Phoenix was building a great nest, the materials of which cast a scent upon the evening air so sweet that Potter moaned. Altogether, he felt a dread to be spying on this splendid presence. He loved him suddenly; but he feared him, too. What if *Felix* should turn an eye and notice Potter? Why, Potter would bow his head and die. See what fine intelligence directed every move the Phoenix made! Nothing was wasted: sticks of cinnamon and—though Potter couldn't name the orient spices—frankincense and myrrh and spikenard, these were the bed of the holy bird. And when all was done, he sighed and settled and rested.

Potter burst into tears.

"Why are you crying, Potter?" whispered the Oriole.

I don't know, said Potter. *He is so old, so tired.*

"Five hundred years old," said the Oriole quietly.

I want to kiss him, said Potter.

"You can't," said the Oriole. "He is attending to a greater work right now."

I know, said Potter. *That's why I'm crying. He is so noble and so lonely, and I wish I were more beautiful—*

Despite their flight, neither of the two friends slept that night, for the air itself trembled with the terrible thing to come. Each time the Phoenix sighed in his nest, Potter's heart jumped.

He said, *Where did Felix come from?*

The Oriole said, "Out of Paradise, my brother, because there can be no dying in Paradise."

9

So far east were Potter and the Oriole that they could see the break of the morning, so close to the early sun that Potter caught his breath and whispered, *Oriole?* The sun was a living being, but one to whom poor Potter couldn't say, *Hello.*

Up the horizon charged the sun, wild and hot and golden. With blasts of the nostril, clattering hooves, he broke the stables, he leaped to the dome of the sky, he ascended, burning, burning. Potter cried, *Oriole?* Some things it is better not to know. What Potter saw, bright in the midst of the fire, was a flaming chariot and four horses each with a shooting eye and the image of a man at the reins. Great were the horses, greater the hands that held them, and terrible the might of the five. But he saw this dimly, as though beaten on a golden dish. *Oriole, was it always this way?*

Potter was frightened.

Then the Phoenix slowly arose on his nest and draped his tail behind. Gravely he watched the coming sun, his colors shimmering. Unmoved he heard the thunder of the hooves. He did not hide. He waited.

When the sun had galloped close above him, the horses straining their necks and the man his shoulders, the Phoenix threw up his head, and the Phoenix began to sing.

Dear God, what a song that was! As though his throat were the pipe of an organ, he made the air to tremble with deep music, woeful majesty at the mouth of the Phoenix and trumpets of supplication. He played pathetic melodies among the baritones, for his memory was long and grievous. Oboes wept and the flutes accused. What did the Phoenix sing? He sang five hundred years of wars. In his song the men went down with bloody strings, and the women hung their heads in

44

elegies, and cannon were the kettledrums between. The Phoenix sang of the sorrow of men, of the fightings and dyings in half one thousand years, and his song was grand, and his song was sad at once.

Stop! screamed Potter, covering his ears. The causes of death were too many for his poor head. *I'm only a boy!*

"A soul," called the Oriole, "and a soul can know the truth!"

But the Phoenix did not sing for Potter. The Phoenix was singing for the sun, and the sun indeed did stop. He reined his chargers backward and dipped a golden ear toward earth, for the song enchanted him. And when the sun stopped, and while the horses stood restrained, the whole world stopped as well: the moon, the stars, and the planet earth all paused in their turning round. Even the angels fell silent. It was a tremendous, mournful thing, all at once to hear the suffering of the people gathered into one sole throat, to hear what the mouth of the Phoenix sang.

As long as the Phoenix uttered his music, the universe held absolutely still.

But then the Phoenix himself gave up the song, too terrible to bear, and bowed his head. Silence. In that moment the sun loosed his reins. The horses felt the slack and bounded up with a greater speed. Their hooves struck sparks from the firmament. The sparks rained burning upon the earth, and they caught in the nest of the Phoenix, and the nest burst into flame. The Phoenix did not so much as raise his head; he seemed to know that this would be the result of his song, and maybe it was the purpose. A sweet, blue fire hissed in the spices beneath him. Smoke closed over him. But the Phoenix kept his head bowed down and did not move.

Felix! screamed Potter. *Oh, Felix, fly away!*

The Phoenix did not.

Instead, his own bright feathers caught fire. His tail became a torch and his wings spread out spilling flames, and he laid his head across the coals and allowed himself to be swallowed in the burning.

And he died.

Poor Potter sobbed and sobbed. Again and again he wailed the sorrow of the mourning dove, unable to look at the char and the smoke arising from the tallest palm tree, and all was silence in the wilderness, save his wailing.

"Hush, Potter," said the Oriole. "This is the story. This is the way that it is supposed to be."

But I loved him, Potter wept.

"And he loved you," said the Oriole.

Oh, Baltimore Oriole, Felix didn't even know me.

"Yes, he did. By name," said the Oriole.

But Potter was brokenhearted. Potter could not be comforted. Was this what he had come to see, the death of a friend greater than his first friend? Potter decided that there was nothing left in all the world, nothing good nor valuable anymore. Death was more real than anything else, so everything else was a lie.

The Oriole said, "Potter, this is not the end of the story."

But Potter neither answered nor looked at his friend. He put his dove's head underneath his wing and determined to hide there forever. *Do you think I care?* Tough Potter. Scornful Potter. Potter the pagan, believing in nothing since nothing was honest at all.

Potter pouted.

A whole day Potter stayed that way, hiding.

The Oriole said, "I brought you to see the story, Potter, and here you are, and isn't it strange that I have to *tell* it to you after all?" Potter didn't answer. So the Oriole said, "There is a worm in the ashes of the Phoenix. Listen. You can hear it stirring."

Tsht. Tshhht. Potter heard the little curling. But Potter did not believe.

On the second day of his pout, the Oriole said, "Oh, Potter, you're missing a miracle. The worm is swelling up. And what was hair, like the hair of a caterpillar, why that is feathers now. This is the story, don't you know."

Potter, twice bereft, saw nothing, because Potter didn't look. A person can pout a long, long time.

On the third day the Oriole scolded him. "Pish, Potter, here is a blockhead for you! The very thing I brought you to see is now before you. The wonder of God is on two legs and his mercy is here in the flesh, and the birds who miss it count themselves unlucky, and that is the most of the birds—but you! You come and stick your nose in your armpit! You mope and miss it. You feel sorry for yourself and so you mock the gift of God. Potter, Potter, the Phoenix is alive again! That's what he comes to show us every half one thousand years, and this is the wonderful end of the story in our own seeing, so that we know, so that we believe it, so that we have hope past our dying. Look at him, Potter! The dead, they do not die forever. Nay! They rise again! Birds by the Phoenix, children by the love of God. Look, Potter, look at the Phoenix. Let the blockhead see and believe."

Indeed, something was different in the world, thought Potter. What it was, it sounded different. Distant noises were gathering, tiny chirps and whistlings, twitters, hoots and downright crows, cackles, cries and lonely scolds, and warbling—

Potter peeped out from under his wing. Behind him, still, was the wide wilderness. But in front of him, high in the top of the tallest palm, stood the Phoenix once again, so beautiful, shaking ash from his royal feathers, young, so young, so strong and free from suffering!

Out of his ashes? whispered Potter. The same love and the same fear kicked at his heart for the sight of the marvelous bird, but harder now since he never thought to see him again.

"Out of his ashes," said the Oriole.

You, Felix! cried Potter, gazing at the eagle eye and ready to burst into tears all over again, but this time for joy. *Oh, you Felix!* he whispered. *How much I love you!*

Potter wanted to fly up into the air. Potter clung to his branch, afraid to lose the vision, because look! Look at the force in the hunch of his shoulders, oh! Look at his glorious crown. And look how he spreads his wings a twelve-foot span, how he slides from the palm, how he strokes and caresses the wind. Oh, look how the thunderbird goes rising up!

Potter began to giggle. He whooped and he plain laughed. His belly tickled at the sight, as though a mountain had kissed him and then had flown. He let go his branch, and without another thought he shot after the Phoenix, higher and higher, and eastward.

Oh, Felix! There was nothing wiser in all the world to do, than to follow the Phoenix eastward. Nobody asked, "Is this right?" They simply did it.

They? They, by the thousands. Birds by the tens of thousands, singing the songs that Potter had heard at a distance. Potter had company!

Out of the green, across the wilderness they came in a rushing multitude, every family and feather, a great cloud of witnesses, a skyborne jubilation! Pigeons and eagles and sparrows flitting; hawks and swallows and geese; thrashers, kingfishers, terns, the shrikes and the crow; tanagers, warblers, larks and the loon, and here and there a dumpy chicken given flight; starlings in overwhelming population; robins, wrens, and cuckoos; pheasant, partridge, turkeys, buzzards, vultures and the owl— a wonderful company, so thick as to darken the earth, and laughing all as Potter laughed, delighted by their holiday, and no one pecking another one. No, these were at noisy peace together. They flew with the joy of life, life not overcome by death. The story had happened again: the Phoenix was their hope, and all their song was "Hallelujah!"

Eastward, eastward sailed the Phoenix. Eastward Potter, too, with never the question *Where are we going?* It didn't matter. He laughed with his friend the Oriole, that was all.

But this day had its ending, too.

For at evening the mighty Phoenix headed into a high and holy wind. It was a good wind, carrying strange and tasty smells and boiling with unearthly color. They did not hate the wind. But it was also a wind of absolute denial, for it blew harder than any bird could fly. Soon ten thousand birds, each beating as quick as it could, stood perfectly still in the sky, while the Phoenix flew on alone.

Where is he going? cried Potter, the screaming wind in his ears.

"Back," called the Oriole. "Back to Paradise, where death can never be, nor tears, nor pain, nor crying anymore."

Can't I go with him?

"Potter, you haven't finished dying yet."

I will miss him.

"But you will remember him," cried the Oriole. Both were cutting the violent current.

Suddenly Potter caught sight of a final wonder. One tiny black bird was drawn into the slipstream behind the Phoenix and followed close at his back. When the Phoenix was swallowed by the lovely cloud, so was this bird sucked in—and there was a flash of red at its shoulder.

Then the wind and the cloud together passed away, and all of the birds were left in a nowhere.

Did you see that? asked Potter.

"Aye," said the Oriole. "I did."

Somebody entered Paradise!

"Aye. Somebody done with dying."

Oh, Baltimore Oriole! Who is so lucky to be with dear Felix forever?

They were floating, now, on an easy wind, the two of them alone, facing westward and the deep green of the evening.

The Oriole said, "What color did that black bird wear?"

Potter said, *Red.*

The Oriole said, "And what was the color of your friend Jonathan?"

Potter smiled. Potter grew thoughtful and older at once. Potter flew on with knowing strokes of the wing. But Potter never answered, because he didn't have to anymore.

He didn't say, *Red.*

10

————

"Fly home, Potter. Fly home as fast as you can."

The song of the Baltimore Oriole had changed. Now it was an urgent pleading and no nonsense: the wonderful story was done, the evening begun. There were important matters of the world to remember, now.

"Fly home."

But I want to stay with the birds, said Potter.

"You are not a bird," said the Oriole.

Feathers! cried Potter. *And flight at the rim of the sky! That's not a bird? And I flew with Felix—*

"Soul of a boy, you are not a bird," said the Oriole.

They were over the sea, two purple specks far behind the westering chariot of the sun.

"And besides all that," said the Oriole, "your mother thinks that you are dead."

Look at me! cried Potter. *I am not dead!*

And to prove it he slipped waterward, a happy dive. He skimmed spume from the ocean till his belly and his balled claws were wet. He soared aloft, performing barrel rolls of magnificent spiral through the air, during all of which the Oriole flew straight forward and no nonsense.

"Potter!" the Oriole called sharply, "you have seen what love is. Now love!"

Then that bird took speed and shot forward in an earnest flight, so that Potter had to cease his foolishness and fly hard in order to catch up.

"Your mother," said the Oriole, "is sad. She is weeping."

Weeping? Crying? said Potter.

"With all of her heart. For you."

For me? Potter asked.

"And why not? She thinks that you are dead, and she loves you, and who's to tell her otherwise but you?"

But I'm not dead!

"So tell her, Potter. Comfort her. Now is the time to share the resurrection. Or would you keep such a wonder to yourself?"

No. Suddenly Potter was worried for his mother, and his heart raced.

"Fly home, Potter. Fly home as fast as you can."

But here came the night behind them. Here came the darkness at celestial speeds, for the sun was so far ahead. Oh, day and night turned faster than wheels on a railroad track, and Potter felt so slow. The night would beat him home. The night would grieve his mother, if he were found dead forever—

Baltimore Oriole, he cried, *how can we fly faster than the night?*

Two dots darting, two birds busy with their wings, two friends, they swooped and sank as God gave them strength. And nobody saw them go. Neither the people below nor the angels above thought anything wonderful in their flight— because who knew the glory they had seen? Who knew it was the soul of a boy midocean and midair? Who knew he went to comfort his mother?

Across the country they sped. The chariot of the sun had long since disappeared. *Wait for us!* cried Potter. *My mother does not understand!* But the sun kept his own schedule. Night had caught up with them, and the air was cold, and Potter was shivering, and darkness lay on the face of the earth. The lights of cities looked like a yellow rash. Rivers were black serpents waiting. Lakes were inky deeps. How lonely was all the land in shadows! How lost its peoples!

Ma-AH-ma! Ma! Ma! wailed Potter. He was so saddened by what he saw after the blazing wonder of the east. And in so vast a territory, how would he find his mother again? *Ma-AH-ma! Ma! Ma!*

"There!" called the Oriole, and he dropped straight down.

Down, too, went Potter, toward the edge of one river, circling round and round until a large two-story house was at the center of his circlings, and the window therein was his own.

"Friends," said the Oriole.

Potter barely heard him. For when he perched on the ledge outside his window and peered inside, his heart broke for the sight before him.

Dim light was in his bedroom. On the bed lay the body of a boy, his mouth wide open as if screaming, but his eyes were closed, and the corpse wore only underpants, and Potter was ashamed. Next to the bed, kneeling, was his mother. Her hands were spread on Potter's chest. Her face was in the sheets. She was crying, crying, shaking her shoulders. And his father stood with his forehead against the wall, and he was crying, too.

Poppi! Who could stand to see his father cry? *Oh, please dear Baltimore Oriole, tell my parents that it is all okay—*

But he heard no answer at his side. Only the wind. The Oriole had gone. Everywhere, over all the lonely world, it was night.

Mama! You shouldn't cry! called Potter. *I am alive!*

At that same moment, his father made a fist. Like a hammer he brought his fist against the wall, once, twice, three times. And then the strong man turned and sank beside the bed of his boy and wailed, "Potter!" and that stabbed Potter to the heart.

He began to beat his wings. He cried *Oooooooo* like a dove. He scratched the broken glass. His father heard the commotion, leaped up and lunged for the window. He threw up the sash and roared, "Go away!" Poor Potter fluttered backward. Then his father ran from the room, and a great pounding began in the depths of the house.

Potter landed on the ledge again. His mother raised her grieving face and said, "Please go away. He can't stand to see birds now—"

But it's me, wailed Potter. *It's only me!*

His father returned with a broom handle. This he thrust out into the night, and he waved it, trying to hit Potter. *Poppi!* "Haven't you done enough?" roared his father. "My son Potter was the best boy that a man could have! Wicked birds! I loved him!" All at once the man sagged on the windowsill, and the broom handle slipped to the bushes below, and he simply wept. "God is my witness," he wept, "how I loved the boy."

Don't, don't, Poppi, don't, cried Potter. He was weeping, too.

Then Potter's mother came to the side of the man, and she knelt down, and she put her arms around him, and she said, "Hush, Papa, hush. The birds could not take our son from us. What do the birds have to do with it? Hush, now. Hush."

They put their faces together, his mother and his father, holding one another. That was Potter's chance. On muffled wings, like the owl, Potter sailed into the bedroom over their heads and landed by the body of the boy. As swiftly as he could, he crammed himself into the open mouth, a cold cave waiting, and he crawled down the throat in such a hurry that he caused a tickling there.

The boy began to cough.

But behold: he was laughing, too.

Coughing and laughing together, the tears filling up his eyes, and watching the faces of his father and his mother, Potter choked, "No, no! But you must love the bird—" That was all he could say. The cough took hold of him and twisted his body all over the bed, and he barked, and he grew pink.

So his father rushed to him, grabbed him, lifted him with a loud shout and squeezed him so that it seemed that his bones would crack.

"Potter, Potter, O Potter!" his father cried with his face to the ceiling. "We thought you broke the window to fly, to go the way that Jonathan had gone. We thought—O my son, my son, Potter!"

The boy felt whiskers deep in his neck and strong arms all around him. He wanted to tell them that the birds praise God, and Jonathan is just fine, and— But he could only cough: the Unstoppable Cough, Potter called it.

His mother was the wise one. His mother had the eyes of understanding. She said, "He did, Martin. He went away. But what does it matter now? He came back to us again." She pushed the hair from Potter's forehead. "And I think you chose to come home, didn't you, Potter?"